HOW-TO SPORTS

HOCKEY

<u>Paul Joseph</u>
ABDO & Daughters

Published by Abdo & Daughters, 4940 Viking Drive, Suite 622, Edina, Minnesota 55435.

Copyright © 1996 by Abdo Consulting Group, Inc., Pentagon Tower, P.O. Box 36036, Minneapolis, Minnesota 55435 USA. International copyrights reserved in all countries. No part of this book may be reproduced in any form without written permission from the publisher.

Printed in the United States.

Cover Photo credits: Superstock
Interior Photo credits: Superstock
Allsport, page 6

Edited by Bob Italia

Library of Congress Cataloging-in-Publication Data

Joseph, Paul, 1970-
   Hockey / Paul Joseph
     p. cm. -- (How-To-Sports)
   Includes index.
   Summary: Explains how to play hockey, briefly discussing equipment, skating basics, team position, and game techniques.
    ISBN 1-56239-647-1
   1. Hockey--Juvenile literature. [1. Hockey.] I. Title. II. Series:
GV847.25.J67 1996
796.962--dc20
                                   96-6105
                                      CIP
                                      AC

Contents

How Hockey Began 4

Equipment 7

Skating... 9

Stickhandling, Passing,

   and Shooting 10

The Ice Rink 16

Hockey Positions 20

Playing the Game 23

Fair Play and Team Spirit 26

Glossary 27

Index 32

How Hockey Began

The game of hockey has been around for many years. Some historians believe hockey was first played in Northern **Europe** hundreds of years ago. It is said that a young boy and some friends were ice skating on a pond. The young boy picked up a long branch and used it to help him balance. He saw a rock and started pushing it with the branch.

The other children with him began doing the same. Soon they set up **goals** and began playing what we know today as "hockey."

Whether or not hockey came to **Canada** from Europe is not known. But the first official hockey game, with written rules, was played in 1875 at McGill University in **Montreal**. These "McGill rules," as they were called, are the basis for hockey rules used today.

Hockey requires many types of equipment.

The game of hockey is very popular in the United States, **Canada**, and Northern **Europe**. It is becoming more popular every year. Because of its fast pace, hockey is a lot of fun. Once players know the basics, they can play the game and see why it is so popular.

Equipment

Before playing hockey, you must have the proper **equipment**. The right equipment will help you play better and avoid getting hurt.

The skates are the most important pieces of equipment. Without skates, you can't play hockey. The skates should fit properly and be sharpened by a professional.

Shoulder and elbow pads protect the player from **checking** and falling to the ice. Shin guards protect legs and knees from the **puck** and **sticks**. Gloves protect the hands.

A mouth guard and a masked helmet must be worn at all times on the ice. They protect the head, face, eyes, nose, and teeth from pucks, sticks, and falls to the ice.

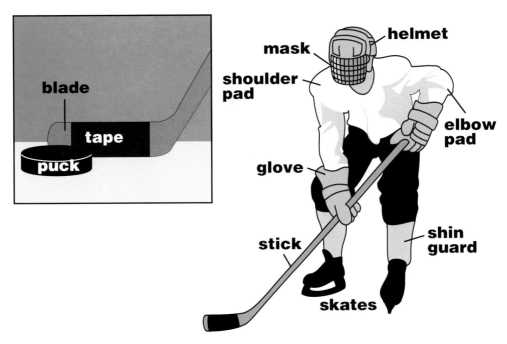

The **stick** should be fitted according to the player's height. Tape the **blade** with special hockey tape to help control the **puck**. The puck is made of rubber and is **shot** at the net to score. Millions of pucks are made each year.

Skating

The first hockey skill to master is skating. It takes a lot of practice to become a fine skater. You must know how to skate in many directions, including forward, backwards, and side to side. A player also must learn to make quick stops and turns.

To skate properly, keep your knees bent and your head up at all times so you can see all around you. Lean forward to keep your weight in front of you for proper balance.

Skates should be sharp and fit properly. To turn, skate, and stop, a skater will use the **blades**' edges.

When a player skates from a standing position, short **strides** are used. Once in motion, longer strides are used to save energy.

The more you practice skating, the better you will become and the more fun hockey will be.

Stickhandling, Passing, and Shooting

Once you have learned the basics of skating, it is time to grab a **stick** and learn how to use it. A stick is needed to **pass** and **shoot** the **puck** into the **goal net**.

To become a good **stickhandler**, you must know how to hold a stick. Place your top hand close to the top of the stick. This hand is the guider and controller.

The bottom hand is the shooting hand, which is usually the stronger of your two hands. Your shooting hand can move up and down, depending on what type of shot you are taking, or if you are stickhandling or passing the puck.

A stick is used to shoot the puck into the goal net.

Stickhandling is to hockey what dribbling is to basketball. When stickhandling, a player skates with the **puck** by guiding it with the **blade** of the **stick**.

As a player skates, he or she must move the puck on the blade from side to side while keeping it from the other team. Always keep your head up and watch where you are going. Never look down at the puck. This will help you keep an eye on the other team, **pass** to a teammate, or take a **shot** at the **goal net**.

Passing is very important to the game of hockey. It sets up the play and most of the goals. When passing, keep the puck on the ice and your hands relaxed. The puck will meet your teammate gently and not bounce over his or her stick.

Opposite page:
A player takes a slap shot.

There are many types of **shots** that a player should learn: the **slap shot**, **wrist shot**, and **snap shot**. The slap shot is used from a long distance. A player takes the **stick** back as far as it can go, then swings quickly at the **puck**, which travels toward the **goalie** very fast.

The wrist shot is taken at close range. A player does not take the stick back very far. This shot is more of a fast flick of the wrist to surprise the goalie.

The snap shot is a combination of a slap shot and wrist shot. It is used from medium range. A player uses the motion of the wrist shot but takes the stick back farther. It is considered by some as a "mini" slap shot.

When practicing different shots, learn when to use them. If you need a quick shot, try the wrist shot. If you have time to shoot, try the slap shot.

A forward stickhandles toward the goalie.

The Ice Rink

The **ice rink** is where the game takes place. It is an ice-covered surface 200 feet (61 m) long and 85 feet (25 m) wide.

Surrounding the rink are walls that are 4 feet (1 m) high. Usually there is glass above them to protect the people watching the game. The walls on the two sides are called **side boards**. The two walls on the end are called **end boards**.

There are two **goal nets** on each end of the rink 10 feet (3 m) from the end boards. This is where players try to score **goals**. The goal net is 4 feet (1.2 m) high and 6 feet (1.8 m) wide.

There are five lines painted on the ice rink that go from side board to side board. There are two red

goal lines where the **goal nets** are placed. There also is a red **center line** that divides the rink in half.

The **blue lines** are on each side of the center line. These lines divide the rink into three different zones called defensive, offensive, and neutral zones.

The five circles painted on the ice are used for **face-offs** at the beginning of a game and after a play is stopped.

How-To
Hockey

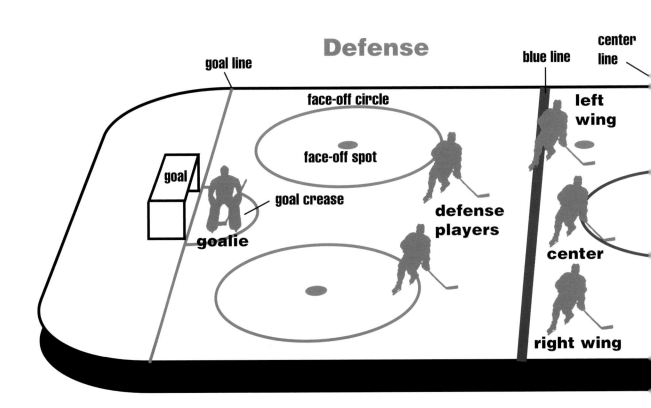

Defense

goal line

blue line

center line

face-off circle

left wing

face-off spot

goal

goal crease

defense players

goalie

center

right wing

Each hockey team plays six players: a goaltender, two defense players, a left wing, a right wing, and a center. The team that controls the puck plays offense. When the team loses control of the puck, they play defense.

Offense

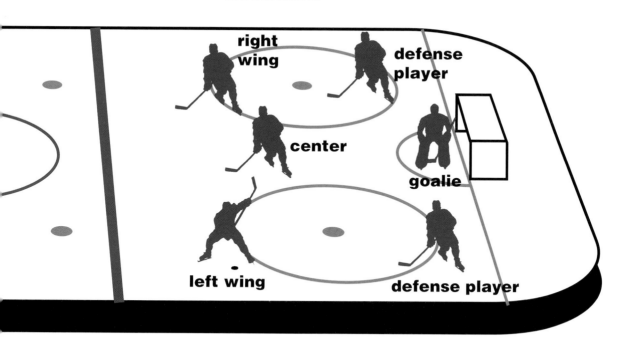

Hockey Positions

Each team has six players on the ice at a time: the **center**, right and left **wingers**, right and left **defense players**, and a **goalie**.

Beginners should learn to play every position. This way they will know which position they play best, and which they like the most.

The center plays between the two wingers. This player is like a quarterback in football or a point guard in basketball. A center must be good at handling the **puck** and directing the team when switching from **offense** to defense. Centers can score **goals**, but their main task is to set up scoring plays with the wingers. Centers also take many **face-offs**.

The **wingers** are on each side of the **center**. Wingers must be excellent skaters and able to receive **passes** from the center. Their main task is to **shoot** the **puck**.

The goalie tends the net.

The two **defense players** play behind the **center** and **wingers**. They must stay close to the **goalie** and make sure opponents don't take good **shots** or get any **rebounds**.

When on **offense**, defensemen play near the **blue line**. They take long **slap shots** or **pass** off to the wingers. Their main job on offense is to keep the **puck** inside the blue line so their team can continue to take shots at the goalie.

Goalies play in the **goal crease** in front of the **goal net**. They must keep the puck from going into the goal. Goalies are considered the last line of the defense. When they stop the puck, they pass it to one of their teammates, or fall on it to stop play. They are the only players on the ice who can use their hands to stop play.

Playing the Game

Now that you know the basics and the positions, it is time to play the game.

Hockey is divided into three **periods**. Periods can last up to 20 minutes. The team that scores the most **goals** after three periods is the winner. If the game is tied after **regulation**, there is an **overtime** period. The first team to score in overtime wins the contest.

The game begins with a **face-off**. The two **centers** from each team stand face to face waiting for the **referee** to drop the **puck** at the center ice circle. Once the puck is dropped, the center who wins the face-off knocks the puck to a teammate.

Hockey takes a lot of practice. Before you begin, get the proper **equipment** and practice the basics.

Begin by practicing your skating. Then grab a **stick** and a **puck** and learn to **stickhandle**. Work on **passing** and **shooting** with a friend.

The more you practice, the easier the game becomes. After awhile you will see why the game has been around so long and why it is becoming more popular every year.

Opposite page:
Practice makes hockey
more enjoyable.

Fair Play and Team Spirit

Every position in hockey is important. Whether a player is on **offense** or **defense**, each position plays a big part in winning or losing a game.

Hockey is a total team sport. No one or two players can win a game. It takes everyone playing together—and playing hard.

Support your teammates throughout the game—no matter how they play. And if you lose, congratulate your opponents. This will make hockey more rewarding—and a lot more fun!

Glossary

blades - the sharp edges on the bottom of skates that a player skates on. Also, the bottom of a hockey stick.

blue lines - two lines on each side of the center line painted blue. They divide the rink into three zones.

Canada - a country in North America, which borders the United States to the north.

center - the player in the middle of the two wingers who set up plays and take the face-off.

center line - the red line in the middle of the ice.

checking - legally blocking a player who has or is trying to get the puck.

defense - the team that doesn't have the puck and is trying to stop the other team from scoring.

defense players - two players that are in front of their goalie on defense and on the blue line on offense. Their job is to help the goalie and pass the puck to the wingers.

end boards - walls on each end of the ice rink.

equipment - the things you must wear or use to play hockey.

Europe - countries such as France, Sweden, and Germany that make up this continent. It is west of Asia and east of the Atlantic Ocean.

face-off - when a referee drops the puck to the two centers who are face to face, to start or restart a hockey game.

goal - shooting the puck into the net and making a score. Also another word for goal net (see **goal net**).

goal crease - the semicircular area at the mouth of the goal net (marked by a red line) where the goalie is positioned. Opponents are not allowed to stand within this crease.

goalie - the player who tries to keep the puck out of his or her team's goal net. Goalies are considered the last line of defense.

goal line - a red line that runs the width of the ice on each side of the rink, on which the goal nets are placed. If a puck crosses this line between the goal posts, a goal is scored.

goal nets - the netted area located 10 feet (3 m) from the end boards where players try to shoot the puck to make a goal and score.

ice rink - the area filled with ice where the game of hockey takes place.

Montreal - the largest city in Canada, which is located in the province of Quebec.

offense - the team that has the puck and is trying to score.

overtime - an extra period used if the game is tied. The first team to score in overtime wins the game.

pass - to push the puck to a teammate.

period - one of three twenty-minute intervals that make up a hockey game.

puck - the disk-like object made of rubber that players try to shoot into the goal net to score.

rebound - a shot that bounces off the goalie, nets, or boards to another player.

referee - the person or people who decide if a hockey rule is broken and what to do about it.

regulation - the time it takes to play three hockey periods.

shoot - to propel the puck toward the goal with the stick.

side boards - walls on each side of the ice rink.

slap shot - a hard and powerful shot often used from long distances.

snap shot - a shot taken at middle range which is between a slap and a wrist shot.

stick - equipment used to shoot, pass, and stickhandle a puck.

stickhandle - guiding the puck with the blade of the stick.

stride - to take long steps.

winger - one of two players on either side of the center. Their main job is to get shots off at the goal net.

wrist shot - a shot taken at close range with the flick of a wrist to surprise the goalie.

Index

B

basics 24
blade 8, 9, 12
blue line 17, 22

C

Canada 4, 6
center 17, 20, 21, 22, 23
center ice circle 23
checking 7

D

defense 20, 22
defense players 20

E

elbow pads 7
end boards 16
equipment 7, 24
Europe 4, 6

F

face-off 17, 20, 23
face-off circles 17

G

gloves 7
goal 4, 10, 12, 14, 16, 22, 23, 26
goal crease 22
goal line 16

goal net 16, 22
goalie 14, 20, 22

H

helmet 7
history 4

I

ice rink 7, 9, 12, 16, 17, 20, 22
injuries 7

M

mask 7
McGill rules 4
McGill University 4
Montreal 4
mouth guard 7

N

net 8

O

offense 20, 22
overtime 23

P

passing 10, 12, 24
periods 23
positions 20, 23
practice 9, 24
puck 7, 8, 10, 12, 14, 20-24

R

referee 23
regulation 23

S

shin guards 7
shooting 4, 10, 14, 24
shoulder pads 7
side boards 16
skates 7, 9
skating 4, 9, 10, 12, 24
skills 9
slap shot 14, 22
snap shot 14
stick 7, 8, 10, 12, 14, 24
stickhandling 10, 12, 24

T

team spirit 26

W

walls 16
winger 20, 21, 22
wrist shot 14